Reycraft Books
55 Fifth Avenue
New York, NY 10003

Reycraftbooks.com

Reycraft Books is a trade imprint and trademark of Newmark Learning, LLC.

This edition is published by arrangement with China Children's Press & Publication Group Co., Ltd.
© Shige CHEN (text)
© Fatatrac, a brand of Edizioni del Borgo srl, Italy (illustrations)
Translation by LeeAnn Geiberger

Educators and Librarians: Our books may be purchased in bulk for promotional, educational,
or business use. Please contact sales@reycraftbooks.com.

This is a work of fiction. Names, characters, places, dialogue, and incidents described either are
the product of the author's imagination or are used fictitiously. Any resemblance to actual
persons, living or dead, is entirely coincidental.

Library of Congress Control Number: 2021918924

ISBN: 978-1-4788-7565-9

Printed in Dongguan, China. 8557/1121/18421

10 9 8 7 6 5 4 3 2 1

First Edition Hardcover published by Reycraft Books 2022.

Reycraft Books and Newmark Learning, LLC support diversity and the First Amendment,
and celebrate the right to read.

illustrated by Pia Valentinis
and Mario Onnis

I Love YOU

ONCE UPON A TIME there was a boy and a girl.

The boy did not speak often. He seemed almost mute.
So the girl constantly spoke to him.

"This is a rose. Smell its perfume!"

"This is a skylark. Can you hear its sweet song?"

"These are clouds. Look, they can fly without wings!"

And the boy nodded as he listened.

However, the boy was really waiting for the
girl to tell him what he most wanted to hear.

One day, on top of a hill,
the girl finally shouted,
"I LOVE YOU!"

Unfortunately, a strong wind was blowing
and it carried her words away. So the boy
thought she hadn't said anything at all to him.
He walked sadly down the hill.

I LOVE YOU I LOVE YOU I LOVE YOU I LOVE YOU

I LOVE YOU I LOVE YOU I LOVE YOU I LOVE YOU

The girl decided to look for her **I LOVE YOU**
that the wind had carried away.

She met a woman working in a field and asked her,
"Excuse me, have you seen my **I LOVE YOU** come this way?"

"What does it look like?" asked the woman.

"It smells sweet, like a rose.
It sings beautifully, like a skylark.
And it flies in the sky as light as a cloud."

"No, I haven't seen it. I'm sorry,"
replied the woman.

But the girl did not give up.

She met a man swinging his legs from
the branch of a tree and asked him,
"Excuse me, have you seen my
I LOVE YOU come this way?"

"Your what?" asked the man, surprised.

"My **I LOVE YOU**," replied the girl.

"Excuse me?"

"**I LOVE YOU.**"

"No, I haven't seen it," answered the man.

Ana moajaba bik

Ya tebya liubliu

Ich liebe dich

Je t'aime

Ég elska þig

Te dua

Main tumse pyar karti hoon

Ne mohotatse

E aroha ana ahau ki a koe

Amo você

Mwen enmen

Ngo oiy ney a

Tsi gě yu i

Sh'teme

Mo konten to

je vous aime

The girl continued on her way.

She walked across plains, she climbed up
mountains, and she sailed over seas,
visiting many countries as she searched.
But she wasn't able to find her **I LOVE YOU**
anywhere...

However, she did meet many of its relatives.

Mi aime jou

Mamihlapinatapei

Te amo

Negligevapse

Ohevet Otach

Ninapenda wewe

Ana ahebak

Ih mwauhkin uhk

Eu te amo

Seni seviorum

In the meantime, **I LOVE YOU** had been
captured by the wind
and begun a long journey around the world.

I LOVE YOU   I LOVE YOU   I LOVE YOU   I LOVE YOU

I LOVE YOU   I LOVE YOU   I LOVE YOU   I LOVE YOU

One day it passed near a house where a baby was crying
and his young mother was trying to calm him.

"Little one, don't you cry," she murmured,
but the baby cried and cried.
At that very moment **I LOVE YOU** flew close to the baby
and whispered into his tiny ear,

"I love you, I love you, I love you…"

Suddenly the baby stopped crying and began to smile.

I LOVE YOU flew by the great mountains of the Himalayas and spied a climber trapped in a cave by a storm of wind and snow. He was curled up in a corner, shaking with cold and repeating, "I'm freezing, I'm freezing."

At that very moment I LOVE YOU flew to his ear and very gently said, "I love you, I love you, I love you…"
The man opened his eyes and suddenly felt strong inside.
He jumped to his feet and said,
"I have never felt warmer and more energetic in my entire life!"

And he left the cave to continue his climb to the peak.

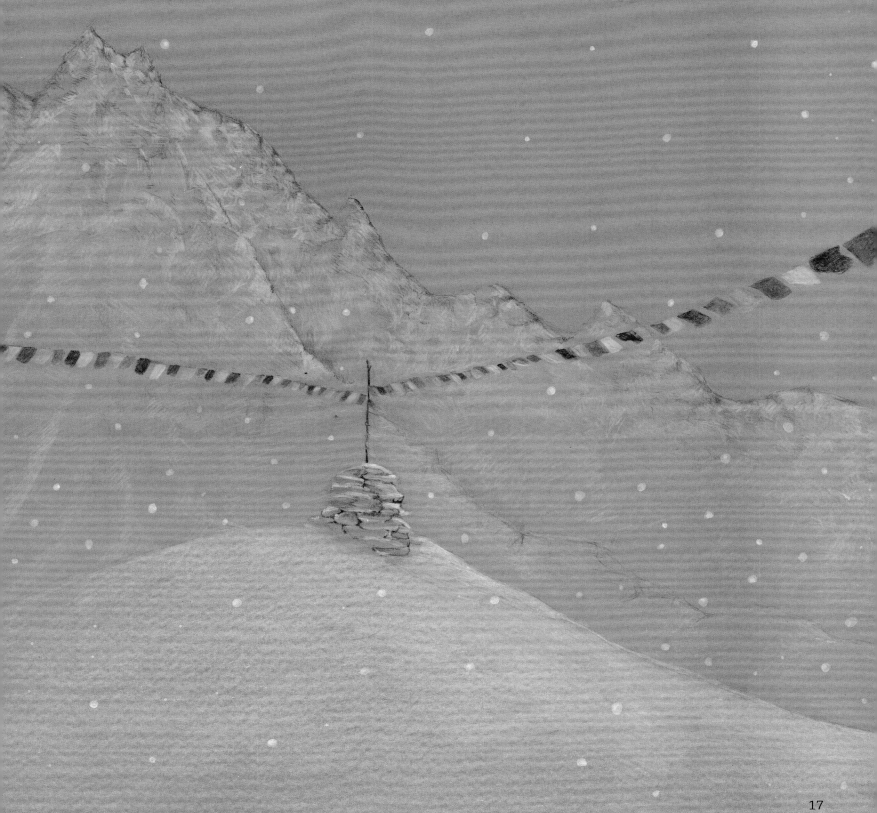

I LOVE YOU flew by a house where an old man lived all alone. He had no more family. His only companion was a little orchid. Watering the plant, the old man stood on his balcony and said, "I talk to you all the time. Why don't you ever answer me?"

I LOVE YOU flew to the old man and whispered, "I love you."

The old man smiled and said to the orchid, "I love you, too."

I LOVE YOU continued its journey and as it
flew over a mountain it called out,
"I love you!"

The mountain raised its head and rumbled,
"I love you!"

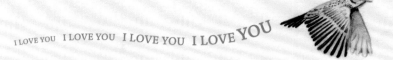

I LOVE YOU   I LOVE YOU   I LOVE YOU   I LOVE YOU

It flew over the forest drenched with rain,
calling out in its loudest voice,
"I love you!"

And the entire forest sang back,
        "I love you!"

I LOVE YOU. I LOVE YOU. I LOVE YOU. I LOVE YOU

It flew over the sea and yelled,
"I love you!"

And the sea swelled its waves and replied,
"And I love you!"

One year later, **I LOVE YOU** came back
to the hill where it began.

It now smelled as fragrant as ripe fruit,
it was as strong as a mountain,
and as energetic as a young horse.

I **LOVE YOU** saw that the boy was still
sitting in the middle of the field.

The boy shone with emotion as he thought
about the girl. At that very moment,
I **LOVE YOU** realized that it had come
to the end of its journey.

Without waiting another minute, it flew very
close to the boy's ear and whispered to him,
"I love you."

I LOVE YOU I LOVE YOU I LOVE YOU

As soon as the boy heard the words, his body shook as if filled with a magical force. At that very same instant the girl appeared before his eyes.

She had grown taller and even more lovely.
She wore a flower in her hair.
But she seemed a little tired.

The boy moved close to her, took her hands in his,
and said, "I love you, too!"

The girl smiled sweetly,
her face illuminated with surprise and joy.

Together
they walked down the hill,
hand in hand.

SHIGE CHEN

is a children's book author and member of the Children's Literature Committee of the China Writers Association. Chen's work has won the National Outstanding Children's Literature Award, the Bing Xin Children's Literature Award, and many others.

PIA VALENTINIS

was born in Italy and has published books all over the world. Her works have won the Andersen Best Illustrator Award, the most important children's book award in Italy. Pia creates her art with a black pen and white paper, then adds color. But she still thinks in black and white.

MARIO ONNIS

was born in Italy, loves reading, making music, and enjoying nature. He graduated from the Fabra Art Workshop.